AN UN~~C~~ NOVEL

THE MYSTERY
OF THE
GRIEFER'S MARK

AN **UNOFFICIAL** GAMER'S NOVEL

THE MYSTERY OF THE GRIEFER'S MARK

WINTER MORGAN

SIMON AND SCHUSTER

First published in Great Britain in 2015
by Simon & Schuster UK Ltd
A CBS company
Originally published in the USA in 2014 by Sky Pony Press

Copyright © 2014 Hollan Publishing, Inc.

The right of Hollan Publishing, Inc. to be identified as the author of
this work has been asserted by them in accordance with sections
77 and 78 of the Copyright, Designs and Patents Act, 1988.

10 9 8 7 6 5 4 3 2 1

Simon & Schuster UK Ltd
1st Floor, 222 Gray's Inn Road
London WC1X 8HB

A CIP catalogue record for this book
is available from the British Library

The Mystery of the Griefer's Mark: An Unofficial Gamer's Novel
is an original work of fan fiction that is not associated with
Minecraft or MojangAB. It is not sanctioned nor has it been
approved by the makers of Minecraft.

PB ISBN: 978-1-4711-4390-8
Ebook ISBN: 978-1-4711-4391-5

Printed and bound by CPI Group (UK) Ltd, Croydon, CR0 4YY

www.simonandschuster.co.uk

TABLE OF CONTENTS

TNT, CRATERS, AND GRIEFERS

I t was a quiet morning as Steve walked through the local village toward Eliot the Blacksmith's shop to trade his wheat for emeralds. Steve had an abundance of wheat because his farm was thriving. Steve loved knowing his supply of wheat could provide him with all the necessities to survive in Minecraft.

"Are you going to use these emeralds to decorate your house?" asked Eliot the Blacksmith.

Steve smiled. "How did you know?" Steve really enjoyed using the emeralds to decorate the walls of his home. He loved the way the green blocks highlighted the grey stone walls. But he also knew that if he kept the emeralds, he could use them to trade with other villagers. "Thanks for the emeralds," he said. "I'll invite you over soon so you can see how they look."

Steve waved goodbye.

On the village street, Steve ran into his neighbor Adam. "Look at all those emeralds," Adam remarked.

"Yes, I just traded them for wheat."

"Well, if you'd like to trade the emeralds, I have a lot of new potions." Adam opened up his chest to display bottles of potions.

Adam was an alchemist who lived with his friend Thomas, an explorer. They were good neighbors to have when you were in trouble because Adam had so many useful potions and Thomas was skillful at fighting off creepers. Luckily Steve hadn't needed their help yet.

"No, thank you. I don't need any potions," said Steve.

Adam wasn't going to take no for an answer. "Really? You don't want a potion of water breathing? If you get stuck in water, you can still breathe."

"I'm never near water. It wouldn't come in handy," said Steve.

"What about a splash potion of slowness? You can use that on your enemies. Do you have any in your inventory? You can really get hurt if somebody attacks you, and it comes in very handy for slowing them down."

Steve thought about his inventory. He didn't have many potions, if any at all. He remembered battling a witch with his friends, Henry, Max, and Lucy, and they had used potions to help them win the battle. The potions had been essential in fighting off the witch.

Steve took out the emeralds. "Okay, Adam," he said. "I'll take the potion of slowness. I hear there is one that lasts eight minutes."

"Yes, it does last that long, and you're in luck because I happen to have it on hand."

As Steve handed the minerals to Adam, he hoped he wouldn't regret this trade.

Adam looked through his chest filled with potions. "That's odd. I thought I had a lot more potions in this chest. I know I had at least three bottles of the potion of weakness, but now I only have one."

"Do you think somebody is stealing your potions?"

"I hope not, but it looks like that is happening." Adam looked through his chest one more time. "Oh no! I don't have any bottles of the potion of harming. I had six yesterday."

"Maybe you traded them and forgot," suggested Steve.

"No, I keep a log of all the potions I've sold. Someone is stealing from me!"

"Who would do something like that?" Steve asked as Adam handed him the potion of weakness.

Adam was angry; he had worked hard to brew all these potions, and he didn't want anybody stealing them. "I bet it's a griefer," he said.

"A griefer?" Steve felt bad for Adam. And he was also worried about himself. If the griefer was attacking his neighbor, he could be next.

"Yes, how else would the potions go missing?" asked Adam.

Steve pointed to a piece of wool on the ground next to Adam's chest. "Look at that. Did you drop wool?"

"No," said Adam as he picked up the wool and broke it in half. "That's odd."

As Steve made his way through the grassy path, he thought about the griefer who had stolen Adam's potions. He wondered if he knew who the griefer was and why that person would steal.

Boom! Steve heard a blast coming from the distance.

Ka-Boom! There was a second blast. Steve sprinted. The sound came from the direction of his wheat farm. He raced toward his home. As he approached, he saw his ocelot, Snuggles, and heard her meowing, but he didn't see his dog, Rufus.

"Rufus," Steve called out, but Rufus didn't come. He called to Rufus again but again Rufus didn't come. Steve was worried about his dog. He walked to his wheat farm and saw Rufus standing by a large crater.

"Rufus!" Steve called out joyfully. As the dog approached, Steve was horrified to see an enormous crater behind him. Someone had blown a large hole on Steve's property. He stared at the hole wondering who would have done this to him, but he was grateful that Rufus and Snuggles didn't get hurt in the explosion. It took a moment for Steve to realize his wheat farm had been destroyed. All his hard work was ruined in one blast. He couldn't imagine how much TNT somebody must have used to blow up his wheat farm.

Nervously, Steve entered his home slowly, looking for TNT in every corner. He was glad his home was okay but was heartbroken over the loss of his wheat farm. Without his wheat farm, Steve didn't have any resources to trade. He was annoyed that he had just traded his last few emeralds for a potion he might never use. Steve knew he had to rebuild the wheat farm, but he didn't have seeds. He needed help. He would have to take the last few emeralds decorating his living room and trade them for resources. He had so many questions. He wanted to find this griefer and ask him why he had destroyed an innocent man's wheat farm.

He looked out at the field where his sheep usually grazed and realized they were all missing! Luckily his cows and pigs were still happily walking about the grassy field.

Steve inspected the rest of the house. He made his way through each room and everything seemed fine.

"At least Snuggles and Rufus are safe and I still have a house. I can always rebuild the wheat farm," he said to himself. Steve wanted to seek revenge on the griefer. He sprinted to his bedroom to get his beloved enchanted diamond sword from his chest. He wanted to suit up in armor and search for the griefer. As he entered his bedroom, he noticed the chest was open.

"Oh no!" screamed Steve as he looked down at the empty chest. Steve's beloved enchanted diamond sword was missing! He had been griefed!

2
OLD FRIENDS, NEW PROBLEMS

Steve looked at the empty chest that had once held his sword and noticed a small piece of wool on the ground. It was just like the wool he had seen next to Adam's chest. But Steve didn't focus on the wool for very long because he needed help rebuilding the farm and finding his sword. He immediately called his treasure hunter friends, Henry, Max, and Lucy, who showed up as fast as they could make it to the farm.

When Steve saw his old friends at the door, he was thrilled, but he was also upset because it wasn't a happy reunion. The last time they were together, they had celebrated their victory over the zombies that had attacked the village. Now they had to find the griefer who had destroyed the wheat farm and get his diamond sword back. But first they had to rebuild. Without rebuilding the farm, Steve would have limited resources.

"Steve, you have no idea where we have been," Henry said.

"We were in the Nether; ghasts were flying above us shooting fire and Max almost fell into lava," said Lucy.

"But then we found treasure in a Nether Fortress. So, it was worth it!" Max said as he placed his diamond sword in one of Steve's chests.

"Guys, someone stole my sword!" Steve blurted out.

"Your sword!" exclaimed Lucy. "How could someone do that?"

"Someone blew up your wheat farm and took your sword?" asked Henry.

Steve nodded yes.

"Do you think you know who did it?" asked Max, pacing as he spoke. "Any suspects?"

"No. I have no idea who would do this to me. But I can tell you that my neighbor Adam is an alchemist and somebody stole his potions. So the griefer isn't just targeting me."

"If the griefer knew Adam had potions

and also knew about your diamond sword, he or she must live nearby. And probably knows you," said Max.

"What about your other neighbor; the house next door?" asked Lucy. "I don't remember it from the last time we were here."

"That's my friend Kyra's house. She's very nice. She traded some wood for wheat recently to help me build an extension to my house. She'd never do anything to harm anyone."

"Did she know you had an enchanted diamond sword?" asked Max.

Steve stuttered his words, "Um. Yes. But."

"Then we have to consider her a suspect." Max said.

"Maybe . . ." said Steve. He shook his head. "But maybe we shouldn't be so concerned with seeking revenge. Let's just focus on rebuilding the wheat farm."

"We will stay with you until the farm is completely rebuilt," said Lucy. "That's what friends do. They help others."

"But we also have to find this griefer," said Henry. "If we don't, the griefer will strike again and other people's stuff will get damaged or stolen."

"And you can be targeted again, too" added Lucy.

Steve knew they were right and they had to find this griefer, not just to seek revenge but also to help others.

It was getting dark and night was setting outside. Two Endermen walked past the window carrying dirt blocks.

"Endermen!" Lucy called out. "They can teleport in here!"

"My house is too high for them to get in. Don't worry." Steve had been extremely thoughtful in planning his home and his life, which is why he was shocked that he was the victim of a griefer.

But before night set in, there was somebody at Steve's door.

Kyra was suited up and standing at his door.

"Don't attack." Steve pleaded.

"I'm not here to attack you. I need your help! Somebody flooded my house with lava." Kyra took off her armor and entered the house. She looked at Henry, Max, and Lucy. "Who are you guys?"

"These are my friends," said Steve, "and they are here to help me. Didn't you notice my wheat farm was blown up with TNT?"

"I don't trust her," said Max. He walked over to Kyra, "How do we know your house was really flooded? And why did show up here in armor if you weren't going to attack us?"

"I don't want to be attacked by hostile mobs. I had to fight a spider jockey on my way over here. It was vicious," explained Kyra.

"There is a griefer amongst us," Steve

announced, "and I can't trust anybody."

"I need a place to stay tonight," Kyra told the group, "Can I stay here?"

The gang looked at each other. They had to trust her.

"Sure," Steve replied. "If you help us find the griefer and rebuild the wheat farm, we will help you with your home. Tomorrow we will break grass to look for seeds to rebuild the farm."

Henry started to tell the folks the plan for finding the griefer. "I'll admit that I used to be a griefer, so I know how they work. I'm sure the griefer is nearby and plotting the next move."

The group made their way to bed. But as Steve entered his room, he screamed out, "Help!" and fell into a deep hole in the middle of his bedroom.

When Steve landed, he lost some hearts and found himself on the ground of a dirt tunnel. There was a chest in front of him. Henry jumped into the hole after Steve.

"Don't open that trapped chest!" Henry yelled. "It's a lava pit trap. If you open it, sticky pistons open up the ground beneath you and you fall into lava."

Lucy, Max, and Kyra jumped into the hole following Henry and Steve.

"What is this?" asked Lucy.

"It's a tunnel." Henry explained. "This is probably how the griefer escaped."

"I wonder where it leads," said Kyra

Steve looked at the tunnel, which seemed never-ending. The narrow dirt walls made him feel trapped. "Let's just go back to my house. It's night and creepers could show up. I want to wait until morning to explore."

Max placed a torch, "We will be fine, and we have some light."

The group slowly made their way through the tunnel.

Lucy noticed a door in the dirt wall of the tunnel. "Look! There's a door! It could be the griefer's house!"

"Let's open it." Henry said.

Max opened the door to the house. They peered in and saw a room filled with lava.

Steve shouted out, "It's Kyra's house!"

"I told you not to trust her." Max told

the group.

Kyra defended herself, "If I was the griefer, would I flood my house with lava?"

"You could be tricking us," said Henry.

Steve closed the door. "This tunnel is very long. It could lead to other homes."

"I'm sure the door to the griefer's house is somewhere in the tunnel," said Lucy.

"If Kyra isn't the griefer." Henry looked at her. He didn't trust Kyra at all.

"We have to trust Kyra." Steve said, and everyone agreed.

As they made their way farther down the tunnel, the light grew dimmer and a skeleton spawned and made its way toward them.

Kyra took out her gold sword and leapt toward the skeleton; with a single blow, she defeated the skeleton.

"If I was a bad guy, wouldn't I just let the skeleton attack you guys?" Kyra questioned the group after her victorious battle with the hostile skeleton.

The group made their way cautiously into the dark tunnel.

"We have to stick together if we want to survive," said Henry.

"I can't believe somebody dug such a long tunnel. It must have taken them a long time," said Steve as they walked. They kept on the look out for hostile mobs that spawned in dark tunnels.

With a small amount of light in the tunnel, Steve walked toward another door. "I wonder who lives in the house," he said.

The gang crept closer to the door.

"I'm going to open it," said Max.

"Don't!" said Kyra, "It's an iron door; it could be a trap."

But Max had already opened the door and they walked through. "Whose house is this?" asked Max.

The door closed behind them. There was no pressure plate to open the door back into the tunnel.

"We're trapped!" cried Lucy.

Dispensers filled with arrows shot at the group as they ducked to avoid being hit.

"It's a booby trap! Duck!" Henry cried out.

Steve narrowly avoided being hit by an arrow that shot close to his head.

"We have to empty the dispensers," said Lucy.

The group was able to stop the arrows. When the flood of arrows stopped, they saw a wooden door. Steve opened it and they were back in the tunnel.

"I've never been so happy to be back in a creepy tunnel," joked Lucy.

"Don't get too confident," said Henry as a cave spider crawled on the wall behind her.

Kyra grabbed her sword again and hit the cave spider.

"I'm impressed." Max said to Kyra.

Keeping their eyes on the walls of the cave, the group carefully made their way through the tunnel.

They stopped in their tracks when they heard something that sounded like rattling bones coming toward them.

Rattle. Rattle. The sound grew louder.

"That sound is too loud, it isn't just one skeleton alone; it sounds like a group of skeletons," Steve said nervously.

From the darkness, the noise grew louder and louder, until the group could see white skeletal bodies advancing toward them.

"Watch out!" yelled Henry as a skeleton shot an arrow at Kyra.

With one mighty blow, Max defeated a skeleton. Lucy and Kyra battled with two skeletons while Henry and Steve battled three.

Henry found a skeleton spawner in the corner. It was a small cage situated by the dirt wall with a tiny skeleton inside its black bars.

"I found the spawner!" Henry announced with excitement.

Henry took out a pickaxe from his inventory and hit the cage with all of his strength and broke the skeleton spawner. The spawner crumbled into pieces and the skeletons could no longer spawn.

With the skeletons no longer spawning, the group was saved! And since Henry broke the spawner, he was rewarded with XP. Getting an XP level meant he now had the power to enchant.

"Good job!" Steve cried out as he raced toward a skeleton with his gold sword. "If I had my enchanted diamond sword, this battle would have been over by now."

Despite having only a gold sword, Steve destroyed the skeleton.

"You did a great job without it, my friend." Henry said as he joined the others to battle the remaining skeletons. When the last of the skeletons were defeated, the group walked farther into the tunnel.

Despite winning the battle, they were still watching for other hostile mobs that could spawn in this low-lit area. It was dangerous, but they were on a quest. They had to find the griefer. They needed to stop this awful tormentor before he caused more trouble.

Steve saw a door off in the distance. "Look, another door!" he said. Steve sprinted toward the door. He ran so fast, he couldn't hear Henry calling out to him, warning him.

"Don't step on that!" said Henry, but

it was too late. Steve had stepped on a tripwire string that opened a hole.

The gang jumped back to avoid plunging into the cavernous hole.

"Thanks for pointing that out, Henry," said Steve. But there was no response.

Lucy called out to Henry, but he didn't reply.

"Henry?!" Steve called out again. But Henry was silent. There was nothing on the ground but a small piece of wool, and no sign of Henry.

Henry was missing!

WHERE'S HENRY?

Lucy was upset. "Where's Henry?" she asked.

"We have to find him," said Max as he placed another torch, "Does anybody see him?"

"He must have fallen down the hole when the pistons activated," said Kyra.

"How are we going to find him?" asked Lucy.

"I'm not sure, but we can't stay here. It's too dangerous. We have to move forward and then make a plan to find him." Kyra started to walk toward the door Steve had pointed out.

"We can't leave our friend, Kyra," said Lucy. "Henry is a part of our team. We can't just abandon our friends when it gets too complicated or dangerous."

"Behind you!" Kyra shouted at Lucy.

Lucy turned around to see a creeper. It let out a loud hiss. Before it could explode, the group sprinted toward the door. When they opened it, they saw Adam.

"What are you doing here, Adam?" asked Steve.

Adam was just as surprised to see them. "This is my house," he said. "I live here. I didn't know there was a door here. This is new."

Steve introduced his friends to Adam and then asked, "Why is there an underground tunnel leading to your house?"

"I don't know. I'm shocked. And to make matters worse, Thomas is missing. I've looked everywhere for him and I'm getting really worried. First, I lose all of my potions, and now I lose my best friend. What is happening?"

"We lost our friend too," said Steve.

"Yes, we lost him in the tunnel," said Lucy.

"And you left without finding him?" Adam asked. He seemed shocked that they would abandon a friend.

"We had to leave, we were being attacked by a creeper," said Kyra.

Just then there was a loud explosion.

"Well, it followed you!" Adam screamed as they ran from the exploding creeper, which had burned Adam's bed.

The group ran to safety in Adam's living room.

"Now that the creeper is gone, I want to go find Henry," said Lucy.

"I'm not going back in that tunnel," said Kyra. "It's a death trap. Adam, you have no idea how many mobs spawned while we were down there, it was tense."

"Do you have another plan?" asked Adam. "If you do, I want to join you guys and also find Thomas. This griefer has to be stopped."

The group could see the sunlight come up in Adam's living room.

"I think it's safe to head home," said Steve. "We have to dig for seeds. My friends are helping me rebuild my wheat farm."

"We have to find Henry first," Lucy reminded him.

"I think I have an idea of where we can look," said Adam. "But first we have to travel to the Nether to get Nether Wart so I can make some potions to help us on our search."

"The Nether?!" Lucy seemed shocked and reluctant to go to this dangerous land. "It will take us even farther from Henry."

"And how can we even trust you?" asked Max, "You could be the griefer and you could be trapping us in the Nether."

"If I was the griefer, would I have stolen my own potions?" Adam asked.

"I'll go, Adam," Kyra told him. "I "know how important it is to have potions when you are going on a dangerous journey." The rest of the group agreed. They needed to find Henry, but going without any potions would be a fool's errand and could cause more harm to them; then they'd never save their friend.

The group followed Adam outside and created a large portal with obsidian, flint, and steel. They emerged into the fiery redness of the Nether.

The gang walked through the landscape filled with lava pools.

Within seconds two ghasts swept through the sky, lunging toward them and throwing a fireball at Adam. He hit the fireball with his sword. It ricocheted toward the ghast, destroying it. The other ghast shot another ball of hot red flames and Max punched the flame as it hit the ghast. They were safe! Ghast tears dropped from the sky.

"These ghast tears are good for potions," Adam said as he picked them off the ground. "But we need to find Nether Wart."

Lucy was excited. "I see a Nether Fortress in the distance," she said, but then she remembered Henry was missing. "Henry is an expert at getting treasure from a Nether Fortress. I wish he was here."

"We'll find him," Max reassured Lucy. "We just need to be prepared and we will be able to save our friend and stop the griefer."

"We do need to go to the Nether Fortress," Adam told Lucy. "It's where you find Nether Wart. I know you miss Henry but maybe we can find some treasure to bring back for him."

"You act like going to the Nether Fortress and finding Nether Wart and treasure is so easy. Last time I was in the Nether, I was battling mobs every second and almost died a million times," said Steve.

"I think you're exaggerating, Steve," said Lucy "It's bad, but it's not that bad."

The minute those words came out of Lucy's mouth, a zombie pigman emerged from behind a lava waterfall. Lucy accidently hit it, provoking the zombie pigman, who charged toward Lucy with a gold sword. The tip of the sword pointed at Lucy's head.

Max raced toward the zombie pigman striking it with great force and saving Lucy.

Lucy sighed with relief. "Thanks Max!"

The gang made their way past pools of lava, watching carefully as they approached the Nether Fortress.

"I see someone entering the Nether Fortress," Kyra said. "We need to get there before that person gets the treasure and the Nether Wart."

"And I think it's Thomas!" Adam shouted to the gang.

5

THOMAS, CAN YOU HEAR ME?

Thomas?" Adam called out in the majestic Nether Fortress, but no one answered.

"Thomas, are you there?" asked Kyra, but again there was no response.

Adam tried again. "Thomas, can you hear me?" Adam sounded defeated.

"Are you sure you saw Thomas?" asked Kyra.

"I'm certain. He was wearing a brown helmet like he always wears when he goes exploring."

"But I thought he was missing," said Lucy.

"He usually tells me when he is going to explore, so I was worried. Especially when somebody stole all of my potions. It just seemed as if somebody was out to get me," said Adam.

"I felt that way too," said Steve.

Suddenly in the distance they

spotted a person in a brown helmet running.

"Thomas!" Adam called out again.

The person sprinted away.

"I guess it wasn't him," said Adam sadly.

"We are wasting time." Lucy told the group. "Henry is missing. Let's just get the Nether Wart and go back to the Overworld."

In most Nether Fortresses, Nether Wart is found along the sides of the stairs, but this Nether Fortress was barren. There was no Nether Wart.

"We need to find another Nether Fortress. The person who was here before us must have taken all of the Nether Wart," said Max.

"Are you sure there isn't Nether Wart in any of the other rooms?" asked Lucy.

"Yes, I checked the other rooms while you waited by the Nether Brick Staircase," said Adam. "This Nether Fortress has been emptied. I'm sure the treasure is gone too. We must find a new fortress."

Looking out on the horizon, they only saw fields of Netherrack and pools of lava. The group was growing weary of this trip to the Nether. It was beginning to seem like a waste of time when they had to save Henry.

"My food bar is very low," said Steve.

"Mine too. I don't think I have enough energy to walk another step, and I definitely can't make it to another Nether Fortress," Kyra added.

"Lucy and I also have low food bars," said Max. "We're almost depleted." One more attack from a hostile mob would leave them with barely enough strength to survive.

"That's why I don't like The Nether," Steve complained. "There's no food here and it can destroy you."

"I still have a lot of energy. I could build train tracks," suggested Adam, "and we can move through the Nether quickly on a train. You can get to another Nether Fortress without you using any food bars."

"A train is a great idea," said Lucy.

Adam started working, using all of his energy to lay tracks and create a train on the Netherrack ground.

The group waited as Adam worked on the train, trying to use as little energy as possible.

"I hope he doesn't take too long," said Lucy, "I want to find Henry."

"We have to be patient," said Steve, "Adam's right, we need to find Nether Wart. This griefer has taken hold of our resources. And who knows how much damage the griefer has done since we've been gone. The griefer could have destroyed my home."

"I don't even have a home," Kyra said glumly.

The complaining came to a halt when a small magma cube jumped toward Max. Its menacing orange and yellow eyes stared at Max as it readied itself for an attack. Max fumbled for his bow and arrow. The cube jumped closer and Max's arrow struck the dark reddish black skin unleashing Magma Cream.

"I have to tell Adam; we can use this cream to brew a potion of fire resistance." Max said proudly.

The victory was short-lived. Seconds later, two more magma cubes leapt toward Lucy and Kyra.

Kyra battled with her gold sword. The cube jumped closer to Kyra.

"Hit it!" Max yelled, "Hit it now!"

Kyra struck the cube, but it didn't destroy the slimy beast.

"Help!" Kyra called out.

Lucy battled the cube with the enchanted diamond sword, but despite having a powerful weapon, the cube was a challenging fight.

"My energy is so low," Lucy said weakly as she mustered up enough energy to battle the cube.

Steve jumped into the thick of the fight with his gold sword, but Lucy gave the cube a hard blow and Magma Cream dripped from the cube.

"Good job!" exclaimed Max.

Kyra struck the cube again, with all the energy she had left, and destroyed the hostile mob.

"We're safe!" Kyra said gleefully.

"But we don't have enough energy to battle any more mobs. This might be the end of us," Steve said nervously.

"No, we'll be fine," a voice called out.

The group looked up to see Adam in a train. "I found a Nether Fortress. Just hop on the train and I'll take you there."

The group made their way into their individual minecarts. The ride to the Nether Fortress felt like a vacation as they looked at lava waterfalls from the comfort of the carts. The group approached the Nether Fortress.

"We're here!" Adam said as they pulled up in front of a large Nether Fortress.

"I hope we don't have to fight any ghasts," said Steve. "If we do, we'll be ruined."

"Let's just run in, get the Nether Wart, and leave. It will be quick," said Adam.

"What about the treasure?" asked Lucy.

"We might have to leave that for another time. Right now, we have to get the Nether Wart."

As the group entered the Nether Fortress, they extracted the Nether Wart growing on the side of the stairs in the center of the Fortress.

"Got it!" Adam collected the last of

the Nether Wart. "Now let's build a portal back home."

As they built a portal back to the Overworld, Steve saw something in the corner of the Fortress tucked away by the Nether Brick wall. He walked over to inspect the corner.

"What are you doing?" Adam yelled. "We need to get into this portal and go back to the Overworld now! Come with us."

Just before Steve ran back to the portal, he took one last look at what lay next to the Nether Brick wall. He could have sworn it was a piece of wool.

The group emerged from the portal to the Overworld in search of food. Lucy saw a pig walking in the grassy field.

"I'll hunt the pig and we can eat." Lucy took out her bow and arrow and skillfully hunted the animal. Using charcoal, she cooked the pig outside Steve's house. They sat by the large crater and feasted.

"I think we can rebuild this wheat farm." Lucy said as she chewed on the food and increased her energy bar.

Max walked over to an apple tree and picked a fresh red apple, "Does anybody want an apple?"

Kyra took a bite of the apple. "I think we all have full food bars now."

Steve looked at the group. "Do any of you have a plan for finding Henry?"

"I think we should go back into the

tunnel. It's our only hope of finding him," said Lucy.

"The tunnel!" Kyra cried out in fear. "I don't think we should go back there. It's too dangerous."

"Henry is our friend and we have to find him," said Lucy, defending her plan. "I will go into the tunnel."

"Your house was destroyed, Kyra. Don't you want to find out who did this? I'm sure once we find the griefer, we'll find Henry," said Steve.

"Let's enter the tunnel from Steve's house," suggested Adam.

Before they could enter the house, dusk began to fall in the Overworld and as the gang quietly finished their food, two Endermen appeared holding blocks.

"Don't look at them," said Max, but it was too late. Kyra had focused her attention on one of the Enderman's white eyes and he teleported towards her.

As Kyra reached for her sword, Lucy struck the Enderman with her diamond sword. It damaged but didn't destroy the Enderman. Max threw a flame arrow and set fire to the Enderman but the powerful monster was still lunging toward Kyra.

Steve ran toward the Enderman, and with all his might he hit the Enderman into the pool of water that sat on the edge of his wheat farm. Steve fell in after the Enderman and swam safely to the shore. As he emerged from the water, Steve realized he had used a lot of his energy to fight off the Enderman.

"Good job," said Adam, "but if you had bought my potion of water breathing, it would have been easier."

As the group walked toward the house, Max accidently glanced at the other Enderman. It teleported toward him. Max took out his diamond sword, prepared to fight but Steve called out, "Run! My house is safe from Endermen. It's too high for them!"

Instead of fighting the energy draining evil creature, Max and the gang sprinted toward the house. As they opened the door, the group fell down a hole in Steve's living room.

Thump! They landed in a new dirt

tunnel.

"Where are we?" asked Lucy.

"It looks like an empty room," replied Max.

"We're trapped!" screamed Kyra.

"We're not trapped," explained Lucy, "let's mine our way out of this room."

Lucy took out her pickaxe and started to break down the wall and the others joined her. As they banged against the wall with hard blows, the group crushed the dirt wall and unearthed a tunnel. There were several doors on the walls of the tunnel.

"I bet the griefer lives behind one of these doors," said Lucy.

"Which one should we open?" asked Steve.

"Let's try this wooden door." Kyra opened the door and found a room with a maze of wool. Wool was stacked around the room, making it virtually impossible to move around the room.

"What is this?" asked Kyra.

"It looks like a wool maze," said Max.

Steve thought about the wool he had seen. Now he knew the wool had to mean something. He was right, the griefer was leaving his mark, but why? Was this all a part of a big puzzle? Would completing this wool maze lead them to Henry?

The group navigated their way through the maze. It was challenging. The wool was stacked as high as the ceiling and the path was extremely narrow.

"Do you think any hostile creatures can spawn here?" Kyra asked fearfully.

"I don't know, but I hope this maze ends soon," said Steve.

They stopped when the maze offered two different paths.

"Which one should we take? Left or right?" asked Max.

"Maybe we should split up," said Adam.

"I don't think that's a good idea," said Steve. "Do you? I mean we might never find each other again and I think it's best if we stick together."

"I just want to get out of here!" Kyra cried out.

Max peeked down the left side, "Let's go left. It seems as if the wool isn't as high on that side. Maybe that's a sign."

Before the group had a chance to respond, Max started to walk to the left and the others followed him.

At the end of the path, there was a door.

"Wow! I chose the right path!" Max called out with joy.

Max opened the door and let out a gasp.

THE ATTACK OF THE RABBIT

They were back in Steve's house. "How can this be?" asked Max as he walked into Steve's house and found all of the beds in the house "destroyed by fire.

"I can't believe the door led to my house!" Steve said in shock. "And the beds! Where are we going to sleep?!"

Lucy was frustrated. "I can't believe we haven't found Henry yet and now we have no place to sleep."

"We can make new beds here or you can all stay at my place," said Adam.

They decided to go to Adam's house instead of making new beds. His house was down the road, and as the gang trekked through the green landscape to the house, they kept a close eye out for hostile mobs that lurked through the Overworld at dusk.

"I wonder what the griefer did to

your house," said Steve as they approached Adam's door.

"I don't care what the griefer did to the house, I just hope Thomas is there."

Just as Adam was about to open the door to his house, Steve shouted out a warning. "Stop!" he yelled. "We have to check for TNT."

Adam and Steve told the others to stay outside as they inspected each room.

"Everything looks good. I can't believe the griefer didn't do anything," said Adam. "But I wish Thomas was here. There's no sign of him."

Steve told the rest of the group the house was safe for them to enter. "We can spend the night here and in the morning we can rebuild Steve's beds."

Night was setting in, and the group needed to sleep. They didn't want to battle any creatures of the night; they had had their fill of adventure that day.

Steve climbed into Thomas's empty bed. He heard a noise, felt something scratching at his feet, and discovered a small piece of wool there. But it was dark, and he quickly fell asleep without telling anyone what he had found. He wasn't sure what all the clues meant, and he didn't want to share it until he could prove Thomas might be the troublemaker who had gotten them into this mess. He also didn't want to blame Adam's roommate and best friend for acts he might not have done. Maybe somebody was setting Thomas up?

The next morning as dawn broke in the Overworld, Adam woke them up from a restful sleep and suggested they head over to Steve's house to help rebuild the beds. "Finally, daylight," he said. "We can build the beds and we don't have to worry about being attacked by monsters."

Max picked an apple from a tree as they walked to Steve's house. He took a bite of the apple. "It's a new day," he said, "and I feel hopeful that we'll find Henry."

Lucy looked off in the distance, "Aw," she said, "look at that cute little bunny in the grass. Does anybody have a carrot? I want to tame it and keep it as a pet."

"If we hunt the bunny, we can have rabbit stew." Max said rubbing his belly.

"And we can also use the bunny to make potions of leaping," added Adam.

Lucy got closer to the bunny, "You guys are awful. It's so cute, I just want to keep it as a pet."

"No!" Steve shouted. "It's hostile and it can kill you!"

"Steve's right!" Max called out. "It's the Killer Rabbit of Caerbannog!"

The white bunny, which looked tame and innocent, was actually a hostile creature and it leapt toward Lucy. Luckily, she was able to sprint away.

Steve shot an arrow at the bunny but it was too fast for any weapon and it was advancing toward Lucy. Unable to kill the fierce creature, Steve built a small brick wall in the bunny's path. The bunny stopped.

"Help me make a cage!" Steve shouted to the group, "We have to trap it!"

Max hid in a corner to avoid the bunny and crafted a cage.

"How are we going to get the bunny

in the cage?" Adam asked as he stood on the wall, high enough to shield himself from a bunny attack.

"We need to lure it into the cage with carrots," said Steve. "You guys distract the bunny and I'll get the carrots."

Lucy and Kyra jumped atop the wall. Then Lucy shot an arrow at the bunny but it hopped to avoid the flinging arrow. Kyra also shot an arrow. The bunny was too busy avoiding the arrows to notice Steve passing by and grabbing a handful of carrots.

"The cage is done!" Max shouted. He placed it next to the wall and then jumped up to join Adam, Kyra, and Lucy on top of the wall.

Steve threw carrots down as he sprinted toward the wall to avoid a deadly attack from this vicious rabbit. Just as the rabbit leapt toward him, Steve quickly threw a carrot into the cage and jumped onto the wall.

The bunny had nobody left to fight. It looked up at the group and then down at the ground, noticing the carrots that lay on in the grass near the cage. It took a bite of a carrot and happily devoured the orange vegetable. Then it hopped toward the next carrot that lay near the cage and ate it.

Steve was excited. "It's getting close to the cage."

"Once it goes in the cage, who will close the door?" asked Max.

"I'll do it," said Adam. "Once the rabbit takes its first bite of the carrot in the cage, I'll jump down and slam the door shut."

They stared at the bunny waiting for it to enter the cage and take a bite of the carrot. It slowly finished the carrot it was chewing.

"I hope it's not full,"said Lucy.

The bunny took its last bite of the carrot and walked toward the cage. Its floppy ears perked up when it saw the carrot lying in the cage.

It cautiously made its way into the cage and took a bite.

Thump! Adam jumped to the ground and with one hand, he trapped the bunny in the cage.

Do you think the bunny could figure out how to break out of the cage?" asked Lucy. "It's so scary and dangerous."

"   "I think it should be fine," said Max, "We need to find Henry. When I was making the cage, I had an idea. Maybe we can set up a trap for the griefer."

"That's an amazing idea!" said Kyra.

"What type of trap?" asked Steve.

"We can create something very valuable that the griefer might want to steal or destroy and we can wait by it until the griefer arrives. Once the griefer shows up, we can trap him and then find Henry."

"That sounds like a great idea," said Steve. "What should we make?"

"I was thinking we could build a small house. The griefer would be curious because it'll be new and there might be valuables in it," said Max.

"Great!" said Kyra. "And then I can live in it once we trap the griefer because I have no home."

"Where should we build it?" asked Steve.

"I think we should build it between your house and Kyra's house. Sound good?" asked Max.

"Yes, let's get started on that right away," said Kyra. She jumped up and immediately walked toward the field where they planned to build the house.

"We need to get some wood," said Steve as they stood on the empty lot where they were going to build the home.

"I have a bunch of wood," Kyra told the gang. "But not enough to make a house."

"Wooden homes are very vulnerable," said Steve. "They can be destroyed by creepers and can burn quickly."

"But we don't want to use all of our resources building a house to trick a griefer," said Adam.

"But Kyra said she might want to live there," said Steve.

"Kyra can live with me until she builds a real home," said Adam. "Right now, we need to focus on the griefer. I need to find Thomas and you need to find Henry, and we all need this griefer to stop destroying everything we create. It will take me months to get all of my potions back."

Max took out a crafting table and started working on the wood for the house. "Kyra's right, we don't have enough wood."

Steve looked at the tree that stood near his property. He always loved looking at the tree from his window, but he knew that if they chopped down the tree, they would have enough wood to make the house. "We can chop down that tree," he said, pointing at the tree.

Adam took out an ax and started to chop down the tree. As Max crafted the house with the wood, Lucy and Kyra built the windows and Steve crafted the beds.

"We don't have to make it very big. Let's just keep it basic," Steve told them.

The group constructed the house,

and when it was finished, they were satisfied with their new structure.

"Not bad!" Max said, walking through the new wooden home. "I might sleep here tonight."

"I wouldn't sleep here. I told you, it is too vulnerable," said Steve.

"I think we'll all have to sleep here tonight," said Adam. "We have to stay here and wait for the griefer. It's the only way we can trap him."

The group had spent so long building the house that they didn't realize it was almost nighttime.

"I guess we have no choice," Steve's voice was shaky, he was scared to sleep in a wooden house—one attack from a creeper and the house could burn to the ground.

"If we stick together, we can make it through the night and maybe the griefer will show up," said Lucy hopefully.

"And what's the plan when and if he arrives?" asked Steve.

Max took out a large cage from behind the house. "I built this earlier. We will trap the griefer in the cage, like we did to the rabbit."

"How are we going to get a person into a cage? We can't lure him in with carrots, he's too smart!" said Steve.

"We are going to take out our swords and tell the griefer if he doesn't surrender, we'll attack." Max had the plan all worked out.

"Do you think that will work?" asked Lucy.

"I hope so," said Max.

Boom! There was a loud blast.

"What was that?!" Max cried out.

"It sounds like it came from the direction of my house!" yelled Steve.

"Should we look out?" asked Lucy. Night was slowly approaching and they knew hostile mobs were lurking on the grassy field.

"We could armor up and see what happened," suggested Kyra.

The group put on their armor and walked out of the small wooden house into the night.

"I don't see any creepers or skeletons," Lucy said as she looked in all directions.

"But look at that! That wasn't here before!" Kyra pointed to a witch hut.

"She's coming out!" cried Max.

The witch's lavender eyes lit up in the dark sky. Her black hat almost blended into the darkness.

"Jump back!" Adam screamed. "She has a splash potion!"

Max took out his bow and arrow and fired at the witch but missed her.

The witch walked closer to the group with a potion in her hand. She took a sip of the potion and raced toward Max.

"She drank a speed potion. Sprint, Max!" yelled Adam.

Max sprinted away but he couldn't move fast enough. The witch threw a potion of weakness at Max and he couldn't sprint any farther.

Steve shot an arrow at the witch, striking her. She fell to the ground.

Adam ran over to Max. "Here's some milk. This will help you combat the witch's potion."

"Thank you," said Max, barely getting the words out because he was so tired.

"Adam," said Steve. He pointed to something in the distance. "Look!"

Adam stood up and looked in the

direction of his home. It had been blown up. "No!" he cried out in despair.

As the sun came up and a new day began, the group could see the side of Adam's house ripped to pieces and the sun beating down on his roofless living room.

9

DON'T GIVE UP

My house!" Adam screamed out in horror. "All my stuff was in there, too."

"Maybe the griefer emptied it out before he blew it up," said Steve.

"That doesn't make things better!" cried Adam.

"When we catch the griefer, we'll make him give back all the stuff he stole from us and you can have all of your potions, too," Steve said hopefully.

"You really believe we'll find the griefer, don't you?" asked Kyra.

"We have no other choice. We must find this evil griefer," said Steve as they walked toward the new house. "Luckily we have this new house. And I'm pretty sure that after what the griefer did to Adam's and Kyra's houses, the new house will be a target."

"Can we look at my house?" asked

Adam. "I want to see how badly damaged it is."

The group quietly followed him to his house. The door was blown off the hinges, and the living room was burnt down, but the back of the house hadn't been touched.

"It's not as bad as we thought," said Steve. "You can still use the bedrooms. All you have to do is rebuild the living room."

"If we could build the decoy house in one day, we can certainly rebuild this one," said Kyra.

The others agreed with Kyra; they would help Adam rebuild his house. Steve looked at the burnt living room and then jumped over the remains of a wall and looked at the devastation around him. On the floor, next to the burnt couch, was a small piece of wool.

Steve picked up the wool. "What is this? I keep seeing wool every time the griefer strikes."

"Do you think it's a sign?" asked Lucy as she took the wool from Steve's hand.

"When the griefer blew up my wheat

farm, he also stole my sheep," said Steve.

"I bet he is using the wool from your sheep!" said Kyra.

"And what about that wool maze?" asked Adam.

"You're right. This has to be some sort of sign, but what does it mean?" asked Lucy.

The group was dumbfounded. They weren't sure what the wool meant. Then Steve said, "I think it's the griefer's calling card."

"What does that mean?" asked Lucy.

"The griefer is using the wool to show that each of these horrible acts was done by the same griefer, and he's taking credit for it," explained Steve.

"Why would somebody want to do that?" asked Lucy.

"You know how griefers act," said Adam. "They are very mean and they want people to know they can pull off such risky and complicated crimes."

Kyra started to cry. "With all of our stuff damaged and Henry and Thomas missing, I feel like just giving up," she said. "It seems like we're getting nowhere."

"We can't give up," said Steve. "We are going to solve this mystery and rebuild."

As the group walked back to the new house, Adam trailed behind them. Just then, he saw someone running past him. "Thomas!" he called out.

The gang turned around, but they didn't see anybody.

"Are you imagining Thomas again?" asked Steve.

"No, I just saw him run by. When I called his name, he seemed to disappear." Adam sounded defeated.

"Why would Thomas do that?" asked Steve.

"I don't know."

"Where did you see him?" asked Steve.

"By that apple tree," said Adam.

Steve walked to the tree and checked for signs of Thomas. Most of the apples had been eaten off the tree. He wondered if Thomas was the griefer and was hiding in the tree and eating the apples to survive. Besides the almost barren apple tree, there was nothing there.

Steve walked slowly to see if there was a hole in the ground. He thought Thomas could be hiding underground, but the grass hadn't been touched.

The sea was just a few feet away. Maybe Thomas stole Adam's potion of water breathing and was living beneath the sea and eating fish. There were so many thoughts swimming through Steve's head and he didn't know how to make sense of them. He just wanted everything to be the way it was before. He wanted his wheat farm back. He wanted to enjoy quiet mornings in the village. He knew his friends thought he was the person who had hope and believed they would find the griefer, but Steve was beginning to doubt they'd ever find the griefer.

Every day seemed to bring more devastation and no clues that could tell them who the griefer was and where he was hiding.

"Are you coming back to the house?" Adam asked Steve.

"We want to start digging for seeds to rebuild your wheat farm," said Lucy.

Steve tried to sound upbeat; he

didn't want the group thinking he had given up hope. "I'll be right there," he said.

He decided to take one more look around the area where Adam had seen Thomas. He walked past the tree, inspecting the ground, and found a small piece of wool.

10

CHICKEN JOCKEY

Steve ran to join the others. "I found another piece of wool by the tree," he told them.

"Do you think all of this wool and your missing sheep is a sign?" asked Max.

"Yes. It has to be," said Steve.

"Once we find the griefer, we will find out about the wool and we'll find Thomas," said Adam.

"And Henry," added Lucy.

"What happens if we find out that Thomas is the griefer?" asked Steve.

"Thomas isn't a griefer!" Adam said angrily.

"Let's not jump to any conclusions," said Lucy, trying to stop the argument. "We won't know who the griefer is until we find him."

"We can't fight about who the griefer is. We need to rebuild Adam's house and the wheat farm," Kyra reminded them.

The group began to cut the grass to search for seeds, but it was harder than they'd expected.

"This is going to take forever!" said Lucy. She had yet to extract one seed.

"Maybe we should try to find grass farther away from your farm," suggested Max.

The group found a lush area of tall grass outside of the village. They carefully broke the grass.

"I found seeds!" Kyra screamed out in joy.

"That's fantastic," said Steve.

"I found them too!" Max had a bunch of seeds.

The gang was excited about their discovery, but they were also growing hungry. Steve suggested they visit his friend Oliver the Village Farmer. "He has melons. If we trade emeralds, we can get melons, and we can eat them and then use their seeds to plant melons."

"Good thinking!" Kyra said enthusiastically, and the group made their way to Oliver's farm.

There were many ripe melons to choose from at Oliver's farm.

"My friends and I would love a few melon slices," said Steve, handing the emeralds to Oliver the Village Farmer.

"I heard what happened to your wheat farm. What a shame," said Oliver as he handed the slices of melon to the group.

"We just found seeds and we are going to help Steve rebuild the farm!" said Lucy.

"That's great. You have good friends, Steve. I hope you guys can rebuild it soon."

The group rested by a tree near Oliver's farm as they took bites from the juicy melons, saving the seeds to plant near the wheat farm. When they were finished, they walked back to the wheat farm and began digging deep into the earth to plant the seeds.

Lucy pointed to a small patch of land by a tree. "Should we plant the melon seeds here?"

"Yes," replied Steve, "and once the melons grow, I'll look at them and think about what great friends I have and how helpful you are."

"We help each other," said Adam. "I think we are lucky to have each other."

The friends agreed as they crawled into the hole the TNT had made and kept digging deep into the dirt and planting seeds. But then dusk began to set in.

"We need to finish up here. It's too dangerous now that it's getting dark," Adam told the group.

" Rufus barked and startled the group.

"I don't like the sound of that!" said Steve. "It sounds like Rufus is in trouble."

Steve crawled out the hole and everyone else followed.

"What's the problem Rufus? Are you okay?" Steve asked, but before he could check on the dog, he heard a shriek.

"Help!"

It was Lucy!

A chicken jockey stood inches from her feet. The baby zombie riding a chicken clutched a sword as it advanced toward Lucy.

"I don't have a sword on me!" she

called to the group.

Max grabbed his diamond sword and lunged toward the chicken. It jumped back and he missed. Steve shot an arrow at the chicken but the baby zombie deflected it with its sword.

Lucy tried to sprint but the chicken jockey was similar to a shadow; she couldn't move fast enough to escape the green-headed jockey. Max jumped and landed behind the beast, throwing the zombie off the chicken with a heavy blow from his sword.

The zombie fell hard on the ground.

"I defeated it!" Max called out, but before they could celebrate the victory, another chicken jockey cornered Adam.

Adam's gold sword was no match for the black-eyed zombie. It threw Adam to the ground and his sword landed next to him.

Steve grabbed Adam's sword and struck the zombie.

"Got it!" Steve was excited.

"I think we should get inside before more mobs show up. It's getting dark and we're tired," said Lucy, and they sprinted toward their new little house.

As they got into their beds, Lucy asked the group, "Do you think we'll find Henry?"

"I hope so," said Max.

"Hope?" Steve was upset. "Of course we will find Henry. We *have* to find him."

When they woke up, Steve hopped down from his bed and fell right into another hole. He brushed off the dirt, looked up, and found his friends standing next to him.

"Another hole!" said Max.

"I guess the griefer dug it while we were sleeping." Steve said, looking down the narrow path.

"I don't see any doors," said Max.

"I think we're trapped!" cried Lucy.

Steve looked up, somebody had placed a large rock over the entrance to their home.

"How are we going to get out?" asked Adam as a cave spider crawled up behind him.

"Adam, watch out!" said Lucy.

Kyra knocked the spider off the wall with her sword and it fell to the ground.

"This is a death trap. We have to find a way out!" said Adam.

"*Shhh!*" Steve put his finger over his lips.

"How can you tell us to be quiet at moment like this?" asked Kyra.

"Do you hear that?"

They listened and heard a muffled sound coming from the other side of the wall. They put their ears up to the dirt wall and the sound grew louder.

"It sounds like somebody calling for help," said Steve.

"It sounds like Henry!" said Lucy.

11

SLIMES, SILVERFISH, AND SAVING FRIENDS

Henry!" shouted Lucy.

"We're coming to save you!" said Max.

Steve took out his pickaxe and banged into the wall of the tunnel; dirt began to crumble, and a large pile of gravel fell from the top of the wall and landed on the group.

"Stop, Steve!" Adam shouted.

"This isn't going to work," said Max as the gravel came down even faster and it looked as if they were going to be buried in a landslide.

Lucy shielded her head from the gravel that was falling down on the group. "But we have to find Henry," she said.

"We'll find another way," said Steve.

Henry's cries grew louder and the gang realized he was on the other side of the wall.

"Henry?" Lucy called out.

"Help!" His voice boomed through the wall.

"Can you hear us?" Lucy asked.

Henry didn't answer. He just kept repeating "Help."

"At least we're getting closer," said Lucy. "Even though he doesn't know we are trying to save him."

"Oh no!" screamed Steve. As he put his pickaxe down, he realized he didn't just break through the dirt wall in this tunnel of terrors but he'd also cracked open a monster egg and silverfish were slowly making their way out of the cube.

"Watch out!" Adam shouted as a silverfish crept close to his feet.

"Jump up on that pile of dirt," Steve told him. "They can't reach you at that height."

Adam took out a splash potion to kill the silverfish. "Stop!" yelled Max, "Splash potions will attract the other silverfish. Throw gravel on it instead."

Adam took a handful of gravel and threw it at the black-eyed silverfish and instantly destroyed the evil insect.

"There are two more!" Lucy said looking at the silverfish that were creeping toward them. "We have to kill them without waking the others in the egg!"

Max took out his diamond sword and struck one of the silverfish; with one hard blow the silverfish was defeated. Lucy destroyed the other with her diamond sword.

"Good job!" Steve said, sad that he couldn't help. Without his diamond sword, he was unable to fight off many of the hostile mobs they'd encountered. He wanted his sword back, and the quicker they got to Henry, the sooner they would find the griefer and get to the bottom of this chaos. But with a monster egg in front of them which could unleash an infestation of silverfish at any moment, the group had to navigate carefully.

"I'm too afraid to move," Max told the group, as he tried to make his way past the monster egg.

"We have to move further down the tunnel," said Steve.

The group tiptoed past the egg and held their breath as they silently made their way deeper into the dark tunnel.

"We need a torch," said Lucy.

Nobody in the group had one and they all knew this made them incredibly vulnerable.

"I'm scared," said Kyra as the tunnel grew darker and the possibility of being attacked by a creature of the night grew more realistic every second.

"I can't see an inch in front of me," said Steve.

"But I can hear something!" Max called out in terror.

"Henry?" asked Lucy.

"No! Listen!"

Click! Clack! The sound of some creature hopping and landing on the ground echoed through the walls of the tunnel.

"It sounds like slime!" cried Adam.

As they inched their way farther into the tunnel, the sound grew louder.

"Get your stone swords out!" Steve told the group. "We have to battle slimes!"

"I can't see where they are or how

many slimes are there," said Max. He squinted in the dark, but without a torch, he felt like this was a fool's errand. "How are we going to fight them if we can't see them?"

"Just listen!" said Steve. "Use your sense of hearing. When we hear them get louder, we will have to lunge at them with our swords. It's our only hope!" Steve held onto his stone sword with both hands.

Click! Clack! The sound of the slimy creature's gelatinous body landing on the dirt ground was growing louder.

"It sounds like there are two slimes. If there were more, it would be even louder," Max said as he walked slowly toward the sound.

"I think I see light!" Lucy called out.

"That's not light," said Kyra, "it's the reflection from the green slime!"

"They're here!" Max screamed out and struck one of the green slime cubes with his sword and it splashed all over the group.

"Save the slime drops!" said Steve, "They're useful."

Adam plunged his sword into the

other green cube as it hopped toward them.

"Thankfully, we're safe!" Lucy called out.

"Ouch!" Kyra screamed out in pain.

"What happened?" asked Lucy.

"I was bitten by a cave spider!" Kyra said weakly.

Adam gave her milk to combat the venom and Kyra drank it.

"Where's the spider?" she asked.

Before Adam could look for it, he too was bitten. He quickly drank milk as well.

Then Kyra saw the spider crawling toward Steve. "Steve, next to your foot!"

Steve threw gravel on the spider, destroying it.

"We can't keep going down this tunnel, it's getting us nowhere," said Steve.

"And we are getting low on resources," added Lucy, "We need to mine for more minerals so we can trade with the villagers. We need to be prepared for a battle when we rescue Henry."

"But how are we going to get out of here?" Kyra asked as she lay in the corner slowly drinking milk.

"We are going to have to dig our way out," replied Steve.

"Look what happened last time!" protested Lucy.

But before they could argue over the best way to escape, Max called out to the group, "I found a door!"

12
I SPY THOMAS

Open it!" Kyra called out as she regained her strength and stood up.

The group huddled close to each other behind Max as he slowly opened the door. With one foot in the door, Max called out, "This looks very familiar."

The group walked into Adam's house.

"I think we've done this before," Steve joked.

"Whoever is making these tunnels is leading us in circles. They want us to give up," Max told the gang.

Steve looked around Adam's house. "At least the griefer hasn't done any more damage since we were gone."

Adam sighed with relief. "I know, but we still haven't found Thomas or Henry."

Steve inspected the house for holes in the ground. "There might be other tunnels that could get us back to Henry."

"I don't care if you find the biggest hole in the world," said Kyra, sounding exhausted. "I don't think I would jump into it."

As the sky grew darker, the group walked toward their new house, but it wasn't there.

The griefer had used TNT to blow up the house and there was nothing but a large hole in the ground where the home once stood.

"Where are we going to sleep?" Kyra cried out.

"I knew the griefer would target the house," Steve said as he paced, trying to think of a plan. But before he could find the time to come up with a good plan, they heard moaning in the distance.

"Zombies!" Steve shouted.

The group got their swords ready as a group of green-headed zombies crept toward them.

Max fought off two zombies with his

diamond sword. Lucy raced toward a group of zombies and battled them. Kyra joined Lucy. The fight intensified as the zombies fought back with all of their might.

"Take this," Adam yelled as he doused a zombie with a potion of healing.

"Is that a potion of healing?" asked Lucy.

"Yes, it actually harms zombies." Adam said as the zombie started to grow weak and Lucy lunged toward it with her sword.

"It seems like this army of zombies is never-ending!" Max cried out as he battled two zombies with his powerful enchanted sword.

The group fought off the last of the zombies and headed toward Adam's house. They were going to try to sleep, even though the exposed house made them an open target. They had no other choice; their energy levels were growing low and they needed to sleep and get food.

When morning arrived, the gang was surprised they made it through the night without having to battle off any hostile mobs.

"We need food," said Kyra.

"I'll go for a hunt," suggested Lucy.

"I'd like to get some apples," said Steve and he joined her as she went into the fields to hunt for breakfast.

As Lucy searched for chickens, Steve walked next to her. Just then he noticed someone sprint by them.

"Lucy, did you see that?"

"Yes. That was Thomas and he was carrying TNT!"

"I saw the same thing," said Steve. He was worried about how Adam would react. He knew Adam would be devastated when he found out that his best friend was actually the griefer.

Thomas sprinted by again.

"Do you think he saw us?" asked Lucy.

"I'm not sure, but it looks as if he is piling TNT behind the tree by the water," said Steve.

"We have to follow him," said Lucy as she walked toward the tree.

"We can't let him know we are following him. He might try to attack us."

"I have my bow and arrow. I am not afraid of him." Lucy held her weapon tightly.

"If we hurt him, we'll never find Henry," Steve said as they got closer to the tree.

Lucy was angry. "He's caused so much trouble and I want to know why!"

"Shhh!" said Steve as they quietly approached the tree. Thomas wasn't there, but there was a pile of TNT. Steve picked up a few blocks.

"What are you doing?"

"I need to bring this back as proof. Or Adam will never believe us," said Steve. He picked up some more TNT.

Lucy reached over and grabbed a few blocks of TNT as well. "This will also stop him from using it. How can he blow up innocent people's homes?"

"And trap our friend," said Steve as he picked up the last of the TNT.

"He's going to be very upset when he notices his TNT is missing," said Lucy.

"Exactly, it's a part of my plan. When he realizes this is missing, you know he is going to come looking for it. That's when we can trap him and find Henry. And I can finally get my diamond sword back."

"Great plan!" Lucy was impressed.

"Well, I don't know how we are going to trap him. So I only have half of the plan figured out," admitted Steve.

"Well, it's a start," said Lucy as they walked back to the others.

The group was outside eating carrots.

"Where were you guys?" asked Max.

"Where's the chicken?" asked Kyra.

"And the apples?" added Adam.

Finally Kyra asked, "What are you carrying?"

"Is that TNT?" Adam was shocked.

"Yes," Lucy said as she placed the TNT inside the exposed living room.

"Adam," said Steve, anxiously trying to get the words out, "We found Thomas and he was hiding this behind a tree."

"No!" said Adam. "It can't be, you must be mistaken."

Lucy sat down next to Adam and tried to comfort him. "I know he's your friend, but he is the griefer."

"Why would he do something like

this?" asked Adam. But the group had no response. They didn't know what turned Thomas the Explorer into a griefer.

"What are we going to do with all of this TNT?" Kyra asked as she stared at the pile of explosives.

"We're going to trap Thomas," said Steve.

"How?" asked Kyra.

The group was shocked when Adam announced, "I have a plan!"

Adam took the TNT and hid it in his bedroom. "We don't want to make it easy for Thomas. We want him to look for it."

"Do you think he knows we took the TNT?" asked Steve.

"Yes. Who else would take it?" Adam opened his chest where he stored his potions. "It's time for me to use the Nether Wart. I have to brew potions."

As Adam sat at his brewing stand and created a bunch of potions, the group started to rebuild the side of the living room of Adam's house.

Adam came into the living room and told them to dig a hole right by the front door. "When Thomas comes in, he'll fall into the hole."

"You are using his own tricks against him!" Max said as he and Steve put the door on the front of the house.

"Good plan, Adam," said Steve, "That's a great way to trap him."

"Once he's in the hole, I'll be able to use my potions," said Adam.

"But don't forget we need to find Henry," Lucy pointed out.

"Yes, Thomas will lead us to Henry," said Adam.

Bang! A sound boomed from Adam's bedroom.

"What's that?" yelled Steve.

Adam sprinted to his room. His brewing stand was on the floor and all of his potions had spilled onto the floor.

"Thomas is here!" Adam screamed.

They looked for the TNT and found it was still piled in the corner.

"At least he didn't take the TNT," said Steve.

Kyra looked around. "I wonder where he went."

Adam walked over the open window. "I think he ran out through the window."

"He'll be back," Max told the group.

"I know, and we better be prepared," Adam said as he sorted through his spilled potion bottles. "I don't have that much Nether Wart left."

"Do you have enough to make a potion that could stop Thomas?" asked Kyra. "I don't want to travel back to the Nether. I have had my fill of ghasts and zombie pigmen, and I don't want to encounter Magma Cubes. I just want to catch Thomas and rebuild my house."

Adam searched through the chest. "I might have enough potions, but we have to act fast."

"Oh no!" Steve called from the living room. Kyra and Adam ran into the next room to see what was going on.

Steve had fallen down another hole.

"Can you climb up?" asked Lucy.

"Yes, but I don't want to. I can hear Henry. I'm going to save him."

"We're going to jump down and help you," said Max.

"No! Stay at the house. This has to be a trick. He wants us to leave the TNT. I can handle this on my own."

Steve ran down the tunnel toward Henry's voice. "Help me!" Henry screamed.

"Henry, can you hear me? It's Steve." Steve hoped that Henry could hear him, but was doubtful.

"Steve?" replied Henry.

"Yes, it's me. I'm so glad you can hear me!"

"I'm trapped in here."

"How can I get to you?" Henry asked as he dug his pickaxe into the wall and tried to break away the dirt to reach his friend. Soil fell to the ground as he pickaxed the wall. Despite the pile of soil that lay at Steve's feet, he couldn't reach Henry. Steve felt something hard behind the layer of dirt. It was bedrock!

"It's bedrock!" Steve yelled angrily.

"I know!" said Henry from the other side of the wall, "I am being trapped in a bedrock room."

"Do you know how you got there?"

"It was dark, but somebody pushed me into this room when you stepped on that tripwire." Henry sounded weak as he spoke.

"How are you eating?" asked Steve.

"Somebody throws apples in here through a hole in the wall."

"Thankfully you have food."

"But I'm trapped in here."

"I'm going to get you out. I promise."

"How?" asked Henry.

Steve didn't have an answer.

Then Henry said, "The Cube of Destruction."

"The Cube of Destruction?" Steve had never made the Cube of Destruction before and he wasn't sure what to do. It was a powerful cube that could destroy anything. He wondered if it could also destroy them both.

"The Cube of Destruction is the only way you can break though bedrock." Henry told his friend.

"Maybe we can dig above you? How high is the wall?" asked Steve.

"I hear someone coming!" said Henry.

Steve stood quietly and listened. He didn't hear anything. "Henry, are you there?"

"Yes, the person just dropped off the apples," said Henry.

"He must be on the other side of the wall." Steve looked around and didn't see anybody.

"Yes," said Henry, "The hole is on the other side."

"If there is a hole in the wall, I bet that side isn't made of bedrock," said Steve.

"Yes!" said Henry, "I just walked over to the wall and it looks like a small patch is made of dirt."

"If I cut a larger hole in the patch of dirt, do you think you can fit through it?" asked Steve hopefully.

"I think so," said Henry.

"I just have to figure out how to get to the other side of the wall. I bet there is a tunnel that leads there," said Steve.

"Yes, there has to be. It's the way the griefer takes to feed me apples."

"I don't want to leave you," said Steve, "but I have to go. I have to get over to the other tunnel. I think I know how to get there. This griefer has built a series of tunnels all over my town." Steve looked down the long tunnel and wondered if there was a way to reach the other side of the bedrock room through the tunnel. He placed a torch on the wall and walked down the tunnel but it seemed to be a straight line and so he turned back and headed toward Adam's house.

"Please. Come back soon," Henry shouted.

"I promise I will."

As those words fell from his lips, Steve hoped he could keep the promise.

Steve sighed with relief as he climbed out of the hole and saw that the TNT blocks were still piled neatly in the corner. He walked through the house searching for the others.

"Guys," he called out as he walked through the empty house. "Where are you?"

Steve looked at Adam's chest of potions. It was empty. He was nervous. What if the griefer had done something to his friends? Steve sprinted out of the house toward his wheat farm. He hoped his friends were just tending to the land during the daylight hours.

"Max?" Steve called out. "Lucy?"

There was silence. Steve was nervous. How could he save Henry on his own? Now he also had to search for his other friends, too? Steve sprinted into the village and headed to Eliot the

Blacksmith's shop, hoping his old friend might have some news about his missing friends. Maybe they went to see Eliot to get new swords.

The villagers walked about the town. It was bustling. Steve opened the door to Eliot's shop.

"Hey Steve, do you have anything you'd like to trade?" asked Eliot.

"I'm actually here because I can't find my friends. Have you seen Max, Lucy, Kyra, and Adam?"

"No, but there are rumors circulating about you in the village."

"What? What type of rumors?"

"Someone told me you're a griefer." Eliot spit the words out slowly as if he regretted saying them.

"Me?" Steve couldn't believe it.

Eliot nodded.

"But if I was a griefer, why would I blow up my own wheat farm? It doesn't make any sense."

"I said the same thing. But some people started saying you did that in order to trick everyone," said Eliot.

"There's only one way to solve this. I have to find the griefer to prove that I'm innocent. And I also have to find my friends."

Steve left the shop, and as he walked through the village he could hear people talking about him. Everyone thought he was the griefer. He had to find Thomas. He had to find his friends. He had to save Henry. And he needed his diamond sword!

Steve sprinted toward the farm. Rufus barked and Snuggles meowed; they were happy he'd returned. At least they don't think I'm the griefer, Steve thought as he searched through the remains of his burnt home, looking for his friends. Then Steve remembered the TNT. He didn't want to leave the bricks in Adam's house; the griefer could steal it.

Steve made his way toward Adam's house. The door to the house was open. Steve walked in slowly, but screamed "Ugh!" as he fell into a hole.

"We did it!" He heard Lucy calling out happily, "We trapped the griefer!"

Lucy, Max, Adam, and Kyra stood by the hole and looked down.

Kyra looked at Steve. "It's not

Thomas!"

"Steve!" said Lucy, "Where's Henry?"

Steve climbed out of the tunnel. "I found him, but he's in a bedrock room and I can't break through."

"We have to save him," said Max.

"I know," said Steve, "Where were you guys?"

"We were here. We tried to call to you, but you sprinted out of the house so quickly you didn't hear us," said Lucy.

"Have you seen Thomas?" asked Steve.

"No, but someone is telling everyone that you're the griefer," said Kyra. "And we think it's Thomas."

"I know, I was in the village and Eliot told me that everyone believes I'm the griefer."

"We tried telling them you're innocent. But they want somebody to blame," said Kyra.

"We need to find Thomas," said Adam.

"We're going have to split up," said Steve. "Because we can't leave the TNT. Who wants to help me save Henry?"

Max immediately said yes.

Steve and Max set off toward the tunnel, suited up with armor and carrying swords. Weighed down with armor, the walk seemed longer than normal.

"We have to walk quickly. It's almost night," said Steve.

"I know. We also have to watch out for hostile mobs," warned Max.

As evening began to set in, Max shouted, "Skeletons!"

Steve saw four skeletons in the distance.

One of the skeletons shot an arrow at Steve and Max, but they ducked and it fell to the ground.

Steve took out his sword and charged toward two skeletons, narrowly missing a blow from one of the gray, bony, hostile creatures as he plunged his sword into the second one.

The sound of bones rattled with each blow. Max and Steve were outnumbered and had to use all of their skills as swordsmen to survive the battle.

Max's diamond sword was powerful

and he destroyed one skeleton with a single stroke. But Steve was stuggling as he fought with his gold sword. The hits weren't as strong and the battle was exhausting. He needed to save his energy; he had to rescue Henry.

As the skeleton shot an arrow at Steve, Max hit the arrow with his diamond sword, saving his friend. Max then hit the last skeleton and it was destroyed. They were left with arrows.

"   "You saved me." Steve said to Max.

"That's what friends are for. And now we're going to save Henry!" Max said as they walked toward the tunnel.

As the two of them approached the tunnel, they kept a careful watch for hostile mobs that spawned at night. Steve felt more secure with each step they took toward the tunnel. Once they were underground, they would be closer to saving Henry and finding Thomas. As much as Steve wanted to save his friend, he also needed to prove his innocence.

Steve and Max entered the burnt down house and were ready to jump into the tunnel. They looked for the tunnel's entrance, but there was no hole in the ground. The tunnel wasn't there.

15

THE WALL

Where's the entrance?!" Max asked as he looked at the ground.

"Thomas must have filled it in with dirt." Steve said as he took a pickaxe and struck the ground.

"What should we do?"

Steve started digging into the ground. "We need to dig; we have to find the tunnel."

Max and Steve dug deep into the ground but they couldn't find the tunnel's entrance.

"Do you think we should use TNT?" Max asked as they dug.

"I think we'll find it. We just have to dig a little deeper." He paused. "Do you hear that?"

There was a sound of flame igniting.

"A creeper!" Max yelled as the two sprinted out of the house.

The creeper blew up in the house,

while Max and Steve watched in the distance.

"Wow, that was close!" said Max.

"I know!" Steve agreed as they walked back toward the house to search for the tunnel's entrance.

"Look down," said Steve as they stood by the hole they had been digging.

Max looked down. The creeper's explosion revealed a patch in the ground that led to the tunnel's entrance.

"We're going to find Henry!" Steve said as they both jumped into the tunnel.

"Henry," Max's voice boomed through the tunnel.

"Max!" Henry's voice sounded hopeful and excited.

"We're going to save you!" said Steve. "Keep talking so we can find you."

Henry talked nervously, "I'm here. I'm standing by the hole in the wall. I can hear you guys. You're very close."

Steve stopped. He could see a hole in the wall. "I found you!"

Max and Steve started to bang against the wall trying to break through to the other side. Dirt piled up, and they could see Henry's face.

"Guys!" Henry peeked out from his side of the wall, "It's almost big enough for me to crawl through."

The duo worked hard breaking down the wall. They were almost done when they heard someone in the tunnel.

"What's that?" Max asked and stopped tearing down the wall.

"I think it's the griefer," said Henry. "He usually feeds me apples. I'm sure he's bringing me food."

Steve looked at the wall, "Henry, try crawling through. If you squeeze, you can make it."

Henry held his breath as he attempted to squeeze through the narrow hole in the wall. "I think I can do it!"

The griefer's footsteps were growing louder. Steve was trying to think of a plan for their impending confrontation with Thomas.

Henry fell through the hole and landed in front of his friends. It was a brief and joyous reunion. Within seconds they would be faced with the griefer.

Henry, Max, and Steve stood quietly by the hole, trying to hide themselves from Thomas.

As Thomas approached the hole, Steve and the gang jumped in front of him.

"Shocked to see us?" asked Steve.

Thomas sprinted down the tunnel and they chased after him. The group was close on Thomas's trail, but in seconds he had vanished.

"He disappeared!" Steve screamed.

"How did that happen?" asked Max.

"Thomas created these tunnels," said Henry, "and he knows every inch of them. We have to get out of here quickly. I'm sure he has this entire tunnel booby-trapped. We aren't safe here."

They sprinted toward the exit. When they reached the end of the tunnel, they looked up and the hole was gone.

"How are we going to get out of here?" asked Henry.

Steve saw a door at the end of the tunnel, "I think we should open the door."

"No, it could be another trap. I don't

want to be stuck in another bedrock room," said Henry.

"We have no choice. We're going to have to open that door or we're stuck here," said Max.

They held their breath, scared of what they might find on the other side of the door.

Max put his hand on the door and slowly opened it.

They could hear voices. They were deep under the ground and they had to climb their way out of the hole.

The voices got louder. When they finally reached the top of the tunnel, they were shocked to see where they were. They had emerged behind the stack of TNT bricks in Adam's house.

Steve walked out from behind the stack of TNT toward the living room and called out for his friends.

"Steve!" Lucy called out.

Max and Henry entered the living room and the group let out a cheer. They were reunited with their friend.

Steve ended the celebratory reunion when he asked, "Did you know the griefer built a tunnel behind the TNT?"

"No," Adam was shocked and walked into the bedroom.

The others followed him. As they stood by the TNT, they carefully inspected the large hole the griefer had dug.

"When did he build this?" asked Max.

"We never left the house. Maybe he did it while we were sleeping," said Adam.

"He's very tricky," Kyra said. "I never heard him while we were sleeping."

"There is no doubt that he's tricky. Look at how much he's done to us," said Lucy.

Adam looked at the TNT and began counting the blocks.

"What's the matter, Adam?" asked Steve.

"I think some of the TNT is missing."

Lucy looked at the stack of TNT. "You're right. A few blocks are missing."

"I wonder what he's going to do with it?" asked Kyra.

Boom! The sound of an explosion was

heard in the distance. The group sprinted outside to see what the griefer had destroyed.

16
THE GRIEFER

No!" Steve looked at his ruined wheat farm. Thomas had blown it up again.

"After all that work trying to get seeds," said Kyra.

"At least now people won't think I'm the griefer," said Steve. "Why would I destroy my own property twice?"

"I wouldn't be so sure," said Adam. "The villagers might think you're playing a trick."

Steve knew Adam was right and wanted to clear his name. He had to find Thomas. There was no other option.

"We need to trap Thomas," Steve told them. "I have to clear my name."

Steve and the group sprinted back to the house. They didn't want Thomas getting his hands on any more TNT.

As they entered the house, they

could hear a noise in the bedroom.

"It's Thomas!" said Adam. "Let's catch him."

But they weren't quick enough. Thomas made his escape by jumping down the hole.

"Don't follow him!" Steve told them. "It's better if we make our plan here. If we go down to the tunnel, Thomas has the advantage because he knows all of the hiding places."

"He can trap us down there," added Henry. "He did it before."

Deciding on a plan wasn't easy. Everyone had their own opinion.

"I think we should hide the TNT all over Adam's house and we'll trap Thomas as he searches for it," said Kyra.

"I think we shouldn't sleep because Thomas seems to work at night," suggested Max.

But when Adam spoke, Steve and the gang stopped talking and listened. "I think we should use the potion of weakness and have him confess. I know you all want Thomas to pay for his crimes, but Thomas is one of my best friends and there has to be a reason for all of this trouble."

"Adam, you're right," said Steve. "We have to talk to Thomas. Also he's hiding my diamond sword and I want him to tell me where it is. And I want him to clear my name."

The group sat and discussed a plan of action. "Maybe we can take all of our ideas and come up with a master plan," said Steve.

"Yes," Lucy agreed, "I think we have to act fast though. I don't like that the villagers are calling you a griefer. I know they can't attack us, but I bet other people might come here and try to seek revenge."

Steve and the gang decided to dig holes throughout the house. Adam brewed as many potions as he could with his resources. Lucy hunted for food, since the group needed to feast so their food bars would be full. They were going into battle against Thomas and they needed to be prepared.

As they dug their final hole, night was beginning to set.

"This is when Thomas does his griefing," said Adam.

Steve sat on his bed and tried not to

fall asleep. He yawned. *Bang! Clang!* Steve could hear a noise coming from outside the house.

"Suit up guys, we have to see what that is," said Steve.

The group carefully walked outside Adam's house. Adam lit a torch and placed it on the wall.

"Do you see anything?" asked Lucy.

"No," said Max.

Steve could see something off in the distance. It was two sets of glowing purple eyes.

"It's just Endermen," said Steve.

"But they are chasing someone," said Lucy.

The Endermen had teleported and were standing in front of Thomas as he stood with a block of TNT in his hand.

Thomas put the TNT block down and took out a sword.

"That's my diamond sword!" Steve cried. "And I want it back!"

Steve took out his gold sword and sprinted toward Thomas and the Endermen. Despite having Steve's diamond sword, Thomas was being challenged by the two Endermen. The

Endermen made gurgling sounds that were growing louder.

"Help!" Thomas called out.

Steve struck one of the Endermen but the creature wasn't hurt. Steve battled the Enderman as they made their way deep into the grassy meadow. It was dark and he tried not to trip as the Enderman stood next to Steve. The gold sword struck the Enderman. It was getting weaker. Steve knew there was a cliff just a few feet away. Steve fought the Enderman until they reached the cliff and then struck the Enderman and it fell over.

Thomas tried to fight off the other Enderman but he still hadn't destroyed it. Steve joined Thomas in battle and fought off the Enderman. They both fought hard using the gold and diamond swords.

Once the Enderman was destroyed, Steve said, "I want my diamond sword back. You have no idea how hard it was for me to get that sword."

"I'm sorry." Thomas said as he handed the diamond sword to Steve.

Steve held the diamond sword in his

hands. He never thought he would ever be reunited with the sword.

"Why did you do it?" asked Steve, "Why did you steal my sword? Why did you burn down my wheat farm? What did I ever do to you?"

Steve didn't realize how loud he was screaming and it attracted the attention of an army of zombies.

Kyra, Max, Adam, and Lucy sprinted toward the zombies to help their friend. As the group fought off the walking dead with Thomas, they also wondered why he'd betrayed them. And why was he helping them battle off these green-headed beasts? The group led the zombies to the cliff and declared a victorious battle over the night creatures.

As the last of the zombies were destroyed, the group put their swords down. Except Adam; he held onto his sword and walked toward Thomas.

"How could you do this?" Adam shouted and pointed his sword at Thomas.

Thomas stood silently. He had no excuse. He tried to sprint away but

Adam took out his potion of weakness and splashed it on him

As Thomas grew weaker, Steve stood by Thomas with his diamond sword. Now they were going to get answers.

There's a spider jockey behind you."
Thomas said weakly, but Adam
didn't believe him.

"Don't lie to me, Thomas!"

With his last bit of energy, Thomas took out his bow and arrow and shot it at the skeleton.

Adam quickly turned around and hit the spider with his sword, but at the same time his potion of swiftness and his potion of strength fell on Thomas. Adam struck the spider and fell back. Max and Lucy sprinted over to see if he was okay.

"I'm fine." Adam looked over at Thomas, but he was gone. "I accidently let my potions of swiftness and strength splash on Thomas. I'm sorry."

"I don't think he will be that hard to find. We know all of his tricks now," said Steve. "It's not your fault, Adam."

Daylight began to set in and the group walked back to the house to guard the TNT and come up with a plan to find Thomas.

"He's definitely living in an underground house in one of the tunnels," said Lucy.

Baa. Baa. The group walked out of Adam's house to see Steve's missing sheep grazing on the lawn outside the house.

"Do you see Thomas?" Adam asked as he looked around the property.

"He gave back the sheep!" Steve said as he held onto his diamond sword.

"You can put the sword down Steve," Max joked.

"I'm so happy to have it back, I don't want to let go of it," said Steve.

Steve looked at the sheep and realized that Thomas's days of griefing were over. He was using the sheep as a peace offering, but he wasn't sure Thomas was worthy of being forgiven.

The group led the sheep back to Steve's house. Rufus barked and Snuggles meowed when they returned. Rufus walked over to the burnt wheat farm and Steve followed him.

"Guys!" Steve called the gang over, "Look!"

Somebody had tended Steve's land and placed wheat seeds in the soil.

"I bet it's Thomas!" said Adam. "He's trying to make up for all the grief he caused us."

"Maybe splashing him with a potion of swiftness and strength wasn't as bad as we thought," said Kyra.

"Oh no," screamed Max, "Do you think he had something to do with that?" Max pointed to a witch hut just a few feet from the wheat farm.

"A witch!" cried Lucy. She raced toward it with her sword.

"No, use your bow and arrow, Lucy." Max called out. "She can splash you."

But the warning came too late and the witch swiftly splashed a potion of poison at Lucy and she was defenseless.

The witch drank a potion of swiftness, but before the evil creature could sprint toward the group, Max shot her with the bow and arrow.

The group turned to help Lucy who was laying on the ground and were shocked to see that Thomas had appeared and had already raced to her rescue. They watched silently as Thomas handed Lucy some milk. She drank it slowly. "Thank you, Thomas," she said.

As the group walked over to Lucy and Thomas, Adam kept his sword out. He didn't trust Thomas. He felt betrayed by his friend, and despite Thomas's small gestures of forgiveness, he wasn't sure of Thomas's motives.

"I'm sorry," Thomas said as he stood next to Lucy, who was slowly regaining her strength.

But Thomas's words came too late. Adam stood by his friend with a sword.

"Adam," Steve pleaded, "let him explain."

"If you hurt him, we'll never get any answers," said Lucy.

Adam wasn't listening.

18
CONSEQUENCES AND ENDINGS

Adam drew his sword closer to Thomas. "I can't believe you caused so much trouble. Why?"

"I-I'm sorry," Thomas stuttered. "It started out as a joke."

"A joke?" Adam raised his voice.

Steve was angry too. "You have the entire village believing that I'm a griefer and you blew up my wheat farm twice!"

"And you flooded my house with lava!" screamed Kyra.

"You trapped me in a bedrock room!" yelled Henry.

Thomas attempted to defend himself. "I didn't realize how much my griefing was hurting other people and when I finally saw how bad it was, I didn't know how to stop."

"You didn't realize how much you were hurting other people?" Steve didn't believe it.

"It started as a joke; I was just hiding your potions," said Thomas.

Adam was disappointed with his friend. "I don't think hiding potions is funny."

"Truthfully, when you didn't realize I was the one stealing the potions, I wanted to see how many other things I could get away with," Thomas confessed.

Steve was infuriated by Thomas's words. "You weren't thinking of anyone else but yourself!"

"I just wanted to see how much trouble I could cause because I thought it was fun. Then I'd leave the wool. I was waiting for you guys to figure out it was me. And I'm so sorry. I didn't realize it would cause all this trouble. I regret that I took it too far."

"Took it too far?" Adam yelled. "That's putting it mildly."

Steve knew the battle between Adam and Thomas could go on forever. Despite being upset, he said, "Thomas, what is done is done. You're a griefer, but you don't have to stay a griefer. What can you do to change?"

"I gave back the sheep and the sword. I planted the seeds. Can I just say I'm sorry?"

Kyra looked at her home in the distance that Thomas had destroyed. "No, that's too easy," she said.

"I will help rebuild your house," said Thomas.

"I think there's something more important than helping us rebuild," said Adam. "You need to go into the village and tell everyone that you're the griefer. Steve's reputation was ruined and you need to clear his name."

As the group walked into the village, Thomas kept his head down. Steve could see Thomas felt embarrassed. It was a hard thing to admit to everyone, that you were the griefer.

"I know this isn't easy." Steve told Thomas.

Henry couldn't believe Steve was being so kind to Thomas. He was a griefer and deserved punishment. "Why are you being so nice to him?"

"It's hard to admit when you're wrong and Thomas is trying to make things better," said Steve.

The group walked into Eliot the Blacksmith's shop.

Eliot was happy to see them. "Hi guys! Are you here to trade?"

"Not today," said Kyra.

"Thomas has something to tell you," said Adam.

Thomas bowed his head in shame. "Steve isn't the griefer. I am."

"Thomas, why would you do that?" asked Eliot. "And you lied about it, too!"

"I didn't want people thinking I was the griefer," Thomas replied. He couldn't look any of his friends in the eye, but he spoke with genuine regret and remorse.

Thomas walked around the village and let everybody know he was the griefer and apologized. Steve's name was cleared, but Thomas wasn't cleared of his crimes.

Night was beginning to fall, and the group walked back toward Adam's house. Thomas walked at their pace but didn't say a word.

"How do you intend to earn our trust back?" Adam asked Thomas.

"I want to help each of you rebuild what I destroyed, and I will give back everything I stole."

"You stole time away from my friends," said Henry. "How are you going to repay me for that?"

Thomas thought about Henry's question carefully and then responded. "I promise to be the best friend you'll ever have. If you're ever in trouble, I will help you anywhere. If you find yourself stuck fighting the Ender dragon, I'll create a portal in seconds and join you in battle."

"Really?" Henry was still suspicious.

"The one thing that bothered me while I was griefing was watching you guys work together as a team," said Thomas, looking at the group.

"Bothered you?" Steve didn't like the way Thomas phrased his apology.

"Yes, I liked seeing you guys stick together. And I saw how you really cared about each other. It made me feel very bad. I felt so alone."

"But you said griefing was like a game," said Adam.

"Games aren't as much fun when you play them alone. And they aren't fun at all when they hurt other people," said Thomas.

The gang passed Kyra's house and stopped to look at the lava-filled home that had been destroyed by Thomas's TNT.

"Tomorrow I'm going to start rebuilding this house for you," said Thomas. "And I'll make it nicer than your last house. I'm sorry."

Kyra had to trust him. "Okay," she said, "but you can't let us down again, Thomas."

"We need to get to Adam's house before it gets dark," said Lucy and the group hurried on.

Steve opened the door to Adam's house. "It's nice to be able to walk in the door and not worry that we'll fall in a hole and get stuck in a tunnel," he said.

"Or that someone is stealing TNT," added Lucy.

"I'm truly sorry, guys." Thomas felt badly. "I'll never do it again."

"You're a reformed griefer," Steve told him.

Darkness set in as the group was

safely tucked away in their beds. The night was quiet. They didn't need to keep watch for a sneaky griefer and his wool mark. Tomorrow, they'd rebuild. Tonight they could sleep peacefully with their comfortable wool blankets, dreaming of all the fun adventures they'd have now that they didn't have to worry about the griefer.

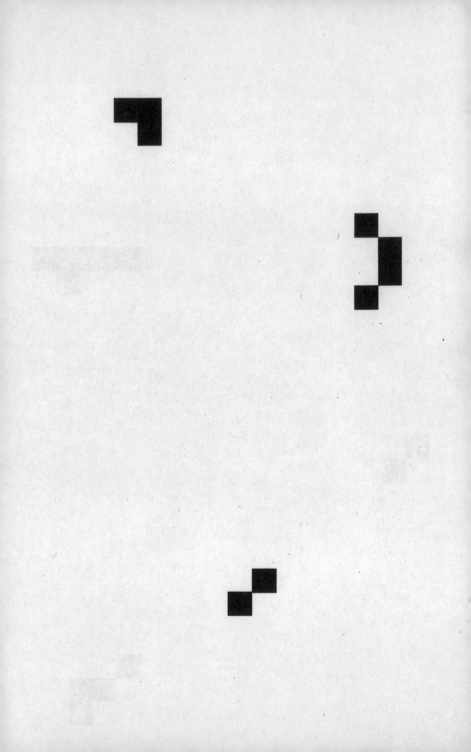

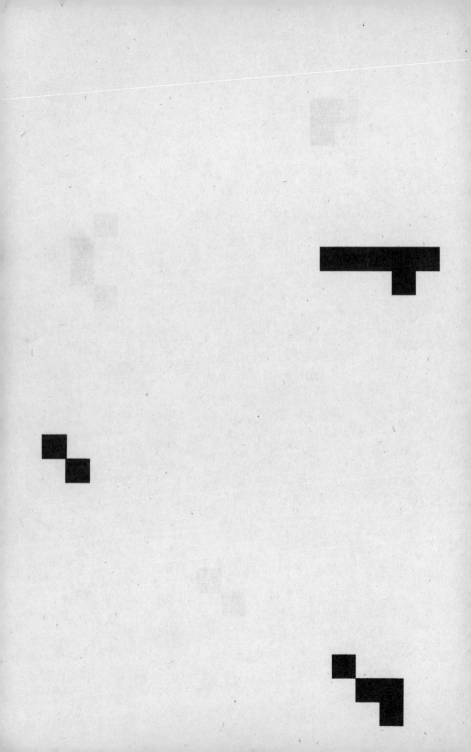

If you haven't read it yet, find out how Steve met his friends in another great adventure!

AN **UNOFFICIAL** GAMER'S NOVEL

THE QUEST FOR THE DIAMOND SWORD

WINTER MORGAN